# MYSTIC MIRACLE

REBECCA HENLEY

# Table of Contents

# Chapter 1

# BLACK CAT SHOP

It was a typical day of the week and two sisters decided to head to the mall. These girls were named Jennifer and Josie. They had not long turned 21. They prepared to head out when the phone rang. "Hi" Josie said. "Hi back" said her caller. Jennifer was getting antsy waiting for her sister to finish on the phone and decided to make a head start. "I'll meet you at the mall" she told Josie, who was giggling like a school girl. Which of course she thought she was.

When Jennifer just got out the door she noticed how beautiful the day was and decided to walk, rather than take the bus or drive. She walked a fair way taking in the beauty that surrounded her. She stopped quite often to smell the roses that had just come into full bloom and to have brief chat sessions with people as they were going about their day, watering their gardens and putting out the trash. She glanced back over her shoulder. Hoping to see her sister catching up. She wasn't there. Jennifer and Josie had been arguing earlier about the company Josie was keeping. She didn't seem to care if she was being taken for a ride. The two sisters were like chalk and cheese. They did however have one thing they liked in common. Shopping!

As she walked along, Jennifer felt like there wasn't a thing that could bring her down today. She felt like she was walking on sunshine and she began to sing as she continued walking. "Josie's always getting herself into trouble" she thought to herself. "She's always doing things she knows isn't right and yet she's oblivious to how he treats her" she thought. "When will she see what it is that he's doing?" Jennifer loved her little sister. She felt, since losing both their parents in a freak accident almost twelve years ago, that she had to be the one to look out for her and to ensure nothing bad happened to her. Jennifer felt that she was the smart one. The one who held it all together and kept them both grounded but, she didn't count on what was in store for her.

When she'd reached the mall she headed in the direction of the Black Cat shop. She knew that there was a range of mysterious and mystical items to peruse. Spell books and all sorts of weird and wonderful things, some of which she couldn't even explain their uses. Whilst waiting for her sister to catch up with her she began looking around the shop.

Jennifer was taking time to sink into the atmosphere of the shop, the smells were delightful, she noticed a spell book on one of the shelves. She picked it up. 'Good Spells for Naughty Little Girls' was the name on the cover. She giggled. From behind her came a voice that said. "Can I help you?" Jennifer was startled, she dropped the book. When it landed on the ground she picked it up and read the page it had flicked open to. 'Attract a Soulmate spell' it read. Jennifer was a little taken aback by this and she quickly replaced the book on the shelf. She couldn't take her eyes off the woman standing in front of the counter. She wore a bright red scarf. An equally bright red beret, she was very pretty, Jennifer noticed. Her outfit was equally in good taste, comprising of a shimmering black blouse with silver sequins and all worn over a lovely, long black, pleated skirt. As Jennifer was a stickler for fashion, good fashion, she approved with a nod of her head in the direction of the woman standing in front of her.

Jennifer took a few steps towards her. She could feel the pull.

"How can I help you?" The woman asked. Jennifer spoke and said "I was just looking" "I found a good little book over there", she pointed to the purple spell book she had dropped earlier. "I was wondering if you could tell me if the spells actually work" she asked her. "Do you believe?" She responded.

# Chapter 2

# SPELLS

The woman headed in the direction of where the purple book was on the shelf. "Do you mean this one?" She asked. "Yes!" Jennifer shifted from one foot to the other. All of a sudden she felt a cold shiver run down her spine. She thought it may have been the front door opening but didn't hear the bell on the door if it had. "Yes!" She repeated. "Do you know if the spells do actually work?" The woman who had, by this time, introduced herself to Jennifer as Catey, spun around on her heels and began to flit around the room, she seemed to be collecting items that Jennifer surmised, were needed to cast one of the spells in the book. "Have you ever cast a spell before?" She asked Jennifer. "No!" "Well yes!" "But only when I was playing around with one that a friend gave me." "You should never 'play around' with any spell" Catey told her. "It could be dangerous if you don't know what you're doing and if you cast it wrong it could be fatal." These words felt like a knife had been pierced through Jennifer's heart. She began to writhe in pain. She had no idea where the pain came from or what it meant but Catey continued collecting. She noticed Jennifer's face had lost its colour. "Are you ok?" She asked. "Yes!" "I'm just a little tired from walking in the sun today." Jennifer decided she was probably heat struck and asked Catey for a glass of water.

Catey stepped behind the door in the corner of the room and Jennifer could hear the tap as she filled a glass with water and returned with it to give to her. "There you go!" "Get that into you and you'll feel much better." Jennifer drank the glass of water, slowly, she did begin to feel better and decided it had to be the heat that affected her. She thanked Catey and set the glass on the counter. "Now!" "Where were we?" She asked. Catey had begun to assemble the items she had collected on the counter. She told Jennifer to take the purple spell book home and cast a spell from it that would attract her soulmate. Jennifer was shocked to hear her say that. This was the exact same spell that the book had fallen open to when she dropped it. "Hmmmmm" she thought to herself. "That's weird!"

Jennifer paid for the book and the items were placed in a bag. Catey didn't charge her for the items, just the cost of the book. Jennifer thanked her and turned to head out the door. "Wait!" Catey yelled. "Hang on a minute!" She grabbed a piece of paper off the top of a notepad and scribbled down something. Catey then walked towards where Jennifer was standing, at the door, handed her the piece of paper and gave her a hug. "Give this number a call" and "Be safe!" She said and gently ushered Jennifer out the door. Jennifer sat down on the seat outside the shop and opened the paper in her hand. It read 'Maurice' and it had a phone number beneath it that looked to Jennifer to be local. She didn't know what to think. She didn't know if she was given Catey's number but she saw that it wasn't her name. She pulled her phone out of her pocket and called it. "Hello?" A woman's voice was heard on the other end. "Who's calling?" Jennifer sat in silence for a few moments as she didn't know what to say. She then replied "It's Jennifer, the woman at the Black Cat shop gave me this number and told me to call it." "Her name is Catey" "Ah Yes!" The woman replied. "What did you say your name was?" "Jennifer" The woman on the other end, who was now known as Louise, told Jennifer that she was expecting her call and she was to visit Maurice at his home. Before she could say anything more the phone cut out and Jennifer thought it had died. It had only ran out of charge. "Damn phone!" Jennifer cursed as she shoved it back in her pocket. "Oh well!" "I don't know where this Maurice lives and what did she mean "expecting her call?" Jennifer thought that Catey may have called her and given her the heads up that she would be calling. "But something isn't right" Jennifer said aloud.

It was then that her sister, Josie, came around the corner. "Jenny" she called. Josie called Jennifer, Jenny. She had done ever since they were little girls playing in the playground at the back of their house. "Jenny" she called again. Jennifer beckoned to her to come over and Josie headed across the road. She suddenly stopped and a car raced past her almost knocking her down. Jennifer didn't see this as she had pulled the book out of the bag and began to read the back of it. She could feel the items Catey had included in her purchase. She glanced in the bag.

There was a small red birthday cake candle, with white stripes, a small bag of pink himalayan salt, a white feather, a small bottle of rose oil and a little plastic bag as well as a small piece of paper and a short black pencil. She closed the bag, looked up and saw Josie heading towards her.

Josie looked like she had seen a ghost. Her face was white, the colour had drained from it and she was panting. "I almost got knocked down" she gasped. Jennifer took her little sister's hand and together they headed into the mall. As they passed by the Black Cat shop Jennifer noticed it was different. It was no longer a shop of mystical, magical, weird and wonderful things, it was now a laundrette. "What the?" She stood bewildered. Jennifer didn't know what to say or do she just kept repeating "How's this possible?" Josie decided that she'd had enough of the mall and suggested they head home. Jennifer agreed.

## Chapter 3

# WHERE THE WIND BLOWS

When Josie and Jennifer reached their gate they stood for a few moments and admired the roses in bloom, which had been planted by their mother. They were beautiful. Jennifer stooped to smell a red one and Josie reached down to pick a white rose that she had been eyeing off as she left the house earlier that day. Jennifer stood back up and felt the book she was carrying, beckoning her to go inside. She opened the front door and Josie and Jennifer stepped in.

Jennifer put her phone on charge and decided to take a quick shower. Josie headed into the kitchen and put the kettle on. "Would you like a cuppa?" She asked. "No thanks!" "I've got something to take care of, you have one and enjoy one for me."

Jennifer disappeared around the hallway corner and into her room. Josie made herself a hot cuppa and sat down to check her text messages.

Jennifer laid out a clean set of clothes on the bed and undressed for the shower. She heard her phone as it dinged many times over from downstairs. "Wow!" "Someone wants me" she laughed and continued to the bathroom. When she had finished showering, Jennifer threw a towel around herself and ducked downstairs to grab her phone. Josie was no where to be seen, however, she did hear a faint giggling and decided that her sister was on the phone. "It's him again!" She retorted. "He's no good for her!" and returned to her bedroom to get dressed.

Jennifer didn't know what she was going to do. She didn't get a chance to finish her phone call with Louise about her visiting Maurice. She didn't know where he lived or who he was. But she felt drawn to meet him. She began to dress. Once Jennifer had donned a pair of old jeans and a rather seductive looking blouse, she headed downstairs, picked up her phone and looked at the messages she had heard earlier, that had been received. There was only 1. She could have sworn the phone dinged heaps of times, indicating there were heaps but it only showed one. It was from Louse.

It read.

42 Champkin Way
Shoulderford

Come when you're ready.

Jennifer had never heard of this area before and searched for it on her phone. "It exists!" She said with a burst of excitement. "I'll head there now." She wasn't quite sure that she was ready but Jennifer wasn't one to turn down an adventure. She left her room, shouted to Josie that she would be home later, got in her car and began to reverse out the drive. Just as she got to the end and almost turned onto the road, Jennifer pulled over. She put the address in her gps and pulled onto the road.

Jennifer noticed the clouds had began to gather and the day seemed to change from sunny and warm to cold and dark and dreary. The wind had picked up and there were spots of rain falling on her windshield. She thought "Wow!" "The weather changed so quickly" it was pouring with rain when she headed off to find the address in her gps.

Jennifer had driven for about an hour when she noticed that the gps had lost service. She tapped the screen on it. It was black. She pulled over and tried to turn it back on but it was dead. "Oh great" "gps has had the dick" she scowled. "How the hell am I going to find this place now?" She drove till she found a roadhouse and pulled in.

Jennifer got out of the car, grabbing her phone and ran inside. "There was a steely looking man standing behind the counter. "Can I help you?" Jennifer walked over to him and showed him the address. "Do you know where this is please?" "Nup!" He replied, quite rudely. "Maybe you should just buy a roadmap or get one of those gps things for your car." He added. "Never heard of that area anyway." "Thank you." Jennifer said and asked if he had a roadmap she might look at. "You gonna buy it?" He asked. "I just want to look at it, is that ok?" "Spose so" he replied and pointed to the books on the shelf across the way. Jennifer took the roadmap book and turned to S for Shoulderford. She couldn't find it. "But the gps found it" she said aloud. "What's the problem?" The rude man asked. "I'm just looking" "it doesn't seem to be here though" Jennifer put the book back and thanked the attendant for his time and for letting her look at the road map, and left. When she almost reached her car her phone dinged with a message.

Just start driving, he'll guide you.

Jennifer read the text on the screen and sat behind the wheel of her car. Something was telling her to drive. She pulled out of the roadhouse and started off. She headed in the direction that felt right to her. Then she turned a few corners and a few more. Before she knew it she pulled over in front of a big house set back from the road. She reversed and pulled into the drive. Jennifer was feeling rather excited for this to be happening to her and at the same time, quite scared. She didn't know what to expect.

The weather had begun to warm up again as she had left the roadhouse and now as she stepped out of the car it had once again taken on the feeling of spookiness. As Jennifer took a few steps towards the front door, the sky went dark. The clouds began to roll rapidly and the wind whipped through the air like a tornado was building. Jennifer couldn't believe the contrast. She ran up to the door just as it was beginning to rain heavily and then she heard the loud clap of thunder and lightning flashed. "We're getting a storm" she thought to herself. But it was fine a short while ago. She knocked on the door.

# Chapter 4

# MERLIN

Jennifer had just about knocked the second time when the door opened. Standing in the doorway was a beautiful young woman. She looked about 25 if she was a day over 18. She was a very tall, thin, woman with long blonde hair that fell down her back and over her shoulders in golden tresses. She looked like she could have been a Hollywood movie star. "Hi" Jennifer managed to say, she was shivering from the cold and couldn't stop shaking. She thought "I'm scared too" "actually I'm petrified" "why did I come here?" "How did I get here?" Jennifer was just about to turn and leave when a young man stepped into the room behind the woman. He disappeared from sight and the woman spoke, "You must be Jennifer" the woman who Jennifer knew was Louise added, "We've been waiting for you!" Jennifer wanted to run but her mind was telling her to "go in!"

Louise motioned to Jennifer to come in and with a swipe of her hand the door closed behind them. The man, Jennifer likened him to the fictional character she knew as Merlin, was sitting in a huge chair in the sitting room. He wore a black cape with a hood that almost concealed his face but Jennifer could see he was young and handsome, with a neatly trimmed moustache above his top lip. She couldn't help thinking "he looks very young and yet he exudes the age of Merlin." "How bizarre." He beckoned to Jennifer to take a seat. Jennifer went to sit down and almost sat on a live frog. She jumped back, startled, 'Merlin' said. "Don't mind him, there's lots of them around this time of year." "These find their way in and never seem to want to leave" He clapped his hands and the frog disappeared. Jennifer could see where it had sat on the chair, there was a small patch of dampness on the cushion. She sat down. 'Merlin' who introduced himself as Maurice began by telling Jennifer that he'd been waiting a very long time for her to arrive. He went on to say that he had been 'told' that she was coming soon, but he didn't know how soon that was. Jennifer told Maurice about the Black Cat shop and how it had disappeared and there was a laundrette there now. He didn't seem to be disturbed by this revelation. Jennifer went on to tell him that the gps had had the dick and that the area couldn't be found in a road map book. He seemed amused by her story. "And yet here you are!" He teased. "Yes!" Jennifer agreed. "Here I am!"

# Chapter 5

# CROSSED PATHS

Maurice began by telling Jennifer that he had summoned her to him as he had information to give to her about her life. Jennifer listened intently. He pulled out a piece of paper and began telling her "at the age of 5 you were sexually assaulted by a family member and then again at the age of 8 by another family member" Jennifer looked at him incredulously. He continued on. "You then left home at an early age and your life began to spiral" Jennifer couldn't believe what she was hearing from this total stranger. "You became involved with drugs, drink and other addictions" "This man knows my whole life" she thought to herself. And listened as Merlin, Maurice told her details of her life as only she could possibly know. He continued "You didn't have a very happy childhood" "you became somewhat involved with shady characters and now!" "You're here!" He went on to tell Jennifer that she had not yet found the one for her and when she did she would break what he called the 3 year cycle. "Every three years something catastrophic happens to you!" "But if you actually opened your heart and your mind, you would see that everything that has happened to you in your life, actually happened for you" "it is all that has happened that has bought you to here" Jennifer sat on the damp seat and wriggled a bit to bring the feeling back into her legs and feet, she had gone completely numb after being told her whole life story by a complete stranger.

He went on to tell her that he wasn't exactly a stranger. He told her that he was standing in the back of the congregation when they lost their parents. He also told her that he was introduced to her when she was a child and he could understand if she couldn't remember. "You were so young" he added. So you see we have crossed paths before. Jennifer sat and stared in disbelief at what Maurice had told her. She glanced around the room and saw that it was covered in a misty cloud which hovered just below the ceiling. She saw the fireplace had a very eerie glow about it and the smell that wafted in from the kitchen was "yuck" she sniffed and gripped her nose with her hand. "That smells terrible!"

Maurice got up and closed the kitchen door. "Louise is cooking again" he laughed. Jennifer laughed with him. "If you take what you have been told and use it to the best of your ability, you will be a success" "if you choose to ignore what I have told you, then you will fail" Maurice got up again and walked over to where Jennifer sat. He dropped down beside her. Placed his hand on her shoulder and Jennifer could feel a strange feeling of calm come over her. She could sense that this man had been bought into her life as someone who would put her on the right track. Jennifer believed everything he told her, especially when he discussed the 'what was to come.' She felt a little strange, to say the least, she didn't quite get why she was feeling that way and she decided that it was time to leave and head home. "Before you go, take this with you" Maurice reached out and touched her hand. Jennifer felt a surge of ecstasy through her whole body. She pulled her hand away. He leant over and took the piece of paper off the little table it lay on. "Here you go!" He had written the pattern of her life in a tunnel type form on the paper. It looked like a spiral of some sort. There were words written inside circles and what looked like a time warp had squiggles and strokes inside it. Jennifer looked at the paper in her hands and said "thank you", but what does this all mean? "This is your life!" He said. "It depicts the cycle I told you about" "if you look closely and study it, you'll find that it shows a pattern" "break the cycle Jennifer." After this Maurice seemed to dissipate right before Jennifer's eyes. She sat rubbing them and pinched herself as to make sure she wasn't dreaming. Louise entered the room. She walked across to where Jennifer was sitting and sat down next to her.

"Did he help you?" She asked. "I think so" "who is he?" Louise began to tear up and she motioned to Jennifer to look where she pointed with a very elegant looking finger which, Jennifer noticed, had a very extravagant, diamond clustered ring on it. "He's there!" Jennifer stood up and walked across the room to the fireplace mantle. "He's here?" She asked Louise. "There!" She indicated a small urn on the mantle piece. "He's been gone for a very long time" "I miss him!" She began to weep. Jennifer turned and walked over to Louise. "He's dead?" Jennifer asked her. "Yes!" "He died in a car accident almost 12 years ago. Jennifer froze. "So did my parents" "I know!" He was the driver of the other car." "He felt responsible for their deaths and he swore, as he lie in his hospital bed, that he would make things right. "He's waited all these years for you to come" then when you happened upon the Black Cat shop he master minded a plan to bring you here. " But the shop doesn't exist" Jennifer corrected her. "No!" Because you're yet to believe. "What about the book and the items I was given from Catey?" "They're at home" "use these wisely" they will bring many blessings into your life, but if you don't learn to believe they'll bring you many curses" Jennifer thanked Louise and crossed over to where the urn stood. "I promise you I'll break the cycle" Jennifer kissed her hand and placed it on the urn. She could have sworn she felt a sudden feeling of love, a warmth, come over her. She headed towards the front door, opened it and stepped outside. She turned to say goodbye to Louise and was shocked to see her standing in the doorway, ready to close the door. She was old. Her long white hair fell over her shoulders and down her back. She was a pale shade of white skinned and her face was wrinkled beyond belief. But she was still beautiful. She could see the ring on the old woman's finger. Before Jennifer could say anything more she closed the door and she heard it lock from the inside. Jennifer pulled her coat across her body and headed to her car.

# Chapter 6

# BRIGHT, SUNNY DAY

The day was beautiful. Outside the sun had begun to shine and there wasn't a cloud to be seen in the sky. Jennifer could feel the warmth of the sun on her face. She reached her car and unlocked it, before she got in, she took off her coat, as it was getting rather warm now and climbed in behind the wheel. Jennifer started the engine and prepared to reverse out of the drive way. She glanced behind her and put the car in reverse. When she looked ahead, as she was about to turn onto the road, she saw the house that she had just left. It seemed to dissipate into thin air. "Hmmmm just like Maurice" she said to herself, "just like the shop" and there in place of where the house once stood was a vacant block of land. No house in sight anywhere. Jennifer pinched herself "ouch!" "That hurt" she whimpered. She realised she wasn't dreaming. She headed the car home.

Jennifer pulled up in the drive way of her house. She got out of the car and headed in the direction of her front door. She thought she saw a shadow duck behind the porch.

She assumed it was Josie. She couldn't help but notice what perfect weather it was. No sign of rain or storm. The birds were chirping in the trees and the wind was blowing gently as it wafted through her hair. Jennifer looked up at the sky and said "it's a beautiful, bright, sunny day and it's just perfect for a spell" she walked up the path, opened the front door and went inside. When Jennifer got to the kitchen she could hear her sister giggling. "Hi" she said as she passed the doorway. "I'm back!" She waved to her sister who was sitting on the back porch in a swing that hung from the rafters. "Sorry I was gone for so long" Josie jumped off the swing and ran inside. "What do you mean?" "Gone for so long" "You were gone all of about 10 minutes"

"What?" Jennifer looked at her watch. "It's stopped!" She whispered to herself. She then looked at the clock on the wall. "She's right!" "I left at quarter to 3 and it's now 5 to" "how's that even possible?" Josie told Jennifer that she was heading over to her b/f's house and that she would not be back until morning. Jennifer told her to stay safe.

Josie asked Jennifer if she could borrow her car as hers didn't have a lot of fuel in it. "Sure!" Josie skipped over to Jennifer, threw her arms around her and gave her the biggest hug. "You're the best sister a girl could ever have" "thanks" Jennifer closed the door behind Josie and headed into the kitchen to make a snack. She was starving. "How could I have been gone for 10 mins?" She asked herself. Jennifer made herself a snack and headed for her room. "Time to cast a spell" she said aloud. Out of the corner of her eye she saw a shadow duck into the dark corner of her room. She dismissed it as the light was playing tricks on her. Jennifer took the book out of the bag and laid the red candle, a small bag of salt, a feather, a small bottle of rose oil and little plastic bag as well as a small piece of paper and a short black pencil on her bed. She stared at them for what seemed like ages. "Ok!" "Now to attract my soulmate" she giggled to herself.

# Chapter 7

# ATTRACT A SOULMATE

Jennifer began to turn the pages. Looking for the one that she saw in the shop. This book held a strange vibe, she decided, it felt like it was "warm." She gasped. The book seemed to be beating, like that of a heart. She could feel it pulsating faster as she turned each page. Jennifer wanted to close it and put it away but something kept telling her to "keep looking" she heard a voice whisper. She wondered if the voice actually came from inside her "but it seems so real" "like he's standing next to me" she had identified it as a male's voice. It seemed familiar. She had heard this voice before but she wasn't too sure where. After flicking through the book she landed upon the words 'Attract a Soulmate.' at the top of the page. "There it is!" She whispered.

Jennifer could feel the presence of someone in the room with her. She kept seeing the black shadow as it flitted in and out of the dark corners of her room. She whispered "Maurice?" She thought it sounded funny but she could feel his presence and a couple of times as she turned the pages she could feel that familiar touch and again it sent a surge of pleasure riveting through her body.

Jennifer stood up and slowly turned around. She half expected to see Maurice standing in front of her. He wasn't there. The slight smell of his house was but he was no where to be seen. She dismissed the thought. "You're just being silly" she told herself and turned back to the spell book. At this time the book was not only beating but it seemed to be writhing on the bed. Jennifer began to read the spell.

Attract a Soulmate Spell

Items needed

1 small red candle with white stripes. (Birthday cake candle can be used).

A small bag of pink himalayan salt.

A white feather.

A small bottle of rose oil

A little plastic bag

A small piece of paper and

A small black pencil

Instructions

Light the candle. Stand it in the bottle of rose oil. Take bag of salt and sprinkle around the bottle in a circle. Making sure both ends meet. Using black pencil, write on paper a description of the man you want to attract. You're soulmate. Be very precise with the list. You will get what you ask for so be specific. Scroll the paper and place it in the bottle with the candle. Blow out candle and waft smoke towards you with feather. Ensuring the smoke touches your face. Pick up pinches of salt and throw around you. Then speak these words whilst doing this.

A Soulmate wish is what I weave.
A list is what I've made.
Now I must believe.
I'll wait for him to come to me.
Don't take too long.
Please hear my plea.

Once the ritual has been performed. Sprinkle rose oil on paper. Place the scroll, the salt and the candle in plastic bag and bury in the earth. Then just wait.

Jennifer followed the instructions to a tee. She was amused with what she was doing. All the while she sensed another presence in the room with her. She sealed the plastic bag with the items inside. She closed the book which had now become lifeless and headed outside. She saw the dark shadow flitting around out of the corner of her eye.

When she reached a place near a tree she began to dig with her hand. A little while down she placed the bag in the ground and covered it with earth. Jennifer stood back up and felt a strange sensation come over her. She was aroused. She could feel her nipples harden inside her bra. The dampness that was gathering inside her knickers was a sure sign of orgasm. She ran inside and locked the door.

# Chapter 8

# THE DARK SHADOW

Jennifer couldn't let go of the feeling that was pulsating though her veins. She was turned on more than she had ever been in her life. She could feel the quivering beginning in her groin and spreading throughout her body. "No one's touching me!" She thought to herself "and yet someone is." She lay down on her bed and beckoned the dark shadow that was loitering in the corner to come to her. She spread her legs and allowed it to take her. Jennifer was writhing in ecstasy when her sister entered the room. Josie couldn't believe what she was seeing. Her sister was lying on her bed and she was having sex with "who?" She asked out loud. Jennifer was startled, the black shadow fled. Josie walked over to the bed and saw the look of sexual satisfaction on her face. "What were you doing?" She asked Jennifer. "It looked like you were having sex" " but there was no one but you on the bed." Jennifer sat up and pulled her blouse around her to cover her now, very erect, nipples. She began to speak to Josie but she couldn't let out a word. She was mute.

Jennifer tried, to no avail, to speak to her sister. Her voice just wouldn't come. She waved her out of the room, stripped naked, closed her eyes and stood in front of the mirror. She opened them. What she saw in the image looking back at her was frightening. She was covered in red welts. They looked like scratches but were deeper, made from very sharp nails, "claws" she said to herself.

Jennifer stepped into the shower alcove and let the water run down her body. She felt the red welts as they stung when the water hit them. She allowed herself to be immersed in the cleansing of what had just taken place. Once she was finished, she wrapped the towel around her and stepped into her bedroom. Passing the mirror and taking a quick glance backwards over her shoulder. The marks were gone. She spoke aloud. "What just happened?" She'd found her voice.

# Chapter 9

# JENNIFER MEETS HER SOULMATE

After a few weeks passed Jennifer had managed to put the whole sexual episode aside. She was standing in the doorway of the local cafe when a handsome, young man walked in behind her. "Sorry" she said as she held the door open. She couldn't help but notice the features of this man. He replied. "No worries" "thanks" Jennifer said "what for?" The man touched her shoulder and she instantly felt a connection. "Wow!" She gasped. "You have the most beautiful eyes" she couldn't stop from saying the words.

"Well thank you!" The man introduced himself as Craig Buttle. "And who may you be?" He asked Jennifer. "I'm Jenny" she replied. A little smirk formed at the corner of her lips. Again she couldn't help but feel that she knew this man. When she sat down with her coffee and cake, he asked if he could sit with her. She waved her hand in a gesture. "Please join me" she said. "I'd love to know more about you!" Craig took the seat next to her instead of the one opposite.

He accidentally brushed against her leg as he settled into the chair. She felt a wave of pleasure wash over her entire body.

"So who may you be?" She asked Craig. She realised the reason that he seemed to be familiar was the list she recalled that lie buried in the earth, near the tree, in her back yard. The little plastic bag that held the items that she used whilst performing the Attract a Soulmate spell. "I live local" Craig began to tell her his life story. She sat glued to her chair and just watched as his luscious lips spoke. She couldn't take her eyes of his face. He wore a black coat with a hood and he had a moustache just above the upper lip. Brown eyes and a very soft spoken voice. She knew she'd found the one. Craig resembled Maurice. Jennifer and Craig sat and chatted the whole day away. He then offered to take her to a movie. She accepted with glee.

After the date had ended and they had exchanged phone numbers Craig walked Jennifer home. He left her on the front porch with a passionate kiss that she knew she'd experienced before. Her mind went back to the day in her room when she was made love to by a shadow. "Craig is the one" she utters as he disappeared around the corner and out of Jennifer's sight.

Jennifer headed to the tree in the back yard. She dug with her hand until she found the plastic bag. She opened it and drew out the piece of paper. Some of the words had faded but she could see some of what she had written.

Must have beautiful brown eyes.
Be quietly spoken.
A few lines she couldn't read.
Must be good in bed.

And the last line read.
Must have a cute moustache.

Jennifer returned the paper to the bag and reburied it. She walked inside and into her room. She lay on her bed and checked her phone. Craig had sent her a goodnight kiss. She sent two back.

The end